Clinton Avenue C

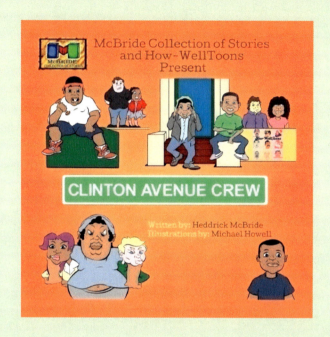

Written by: Heddrick McBride

Illustrated by: Michael Howell

Edited by: Yolonda D. Coleman

Clinton Avenue Crew

ISBN-13:978-1484042762

Peer Pressure

One of the keys to life is making good choices.

You will be confronted by many bad voices.

People will tell you it's cool to do bad things.

Yet, you will have to live with the trouble they bring.

Someone may tell you that you should start smoking.

You will poison your lungs and ruin your teeth; they must be joking.

Maybe you should stay out late, and disobey your parents.

That will never work out no matter how you planned it.

5

Friends may tell you to steal candy from the store.

You have everything that you need, why would you want more?

Don't get caught up in things that you don't want to do

just to fit in with a group or a crew.

They will make you feel bad about getting good grades.

A good report card will help you at any age.

You always have to show others that your mind is strong.

When you make smart choices you can't go wrong.

Find friends who give you some positive thoughts.

They'll make you think about art, music, and sports.

When you remain positive your mind will be fresher.

Just remember to always fight peer pressure.

The Fitness Test

Before you can be strong and perform your best,

You have to pass this simple fitness test.

It starts with stretching; you must try to touch your toes.

The harder you try the farther your body goes.

Then try some push ups where you lift your own weight.

At first it's tough, but later your arms and chest will look great.

Next, go running for a long distance.

You can go as far as you like with any resistance.

In the middle of this test you must stay healthy and be smarter.

Remember to take quick breaks and drink some cold water.

The final part of the test that is most important is to

always play fair and be a good sportsman.

Never cheat to win the game or to be the best.

Give your all at what you do. You passed the FITNESS TEST!

My favorite disc jokey performed at my school.

He played the best music ever, and he made it look cool.

When the party was over, I walked him to his car.

I asked him how I can learn to dj like a rock star.

He said that I had to earn the money to pay for some equipment.
I needed turn tables, head phones, and a microphone in the first
shipment. Later, I can get a mixer and a computer program to
control my music. That way I can scratch, blend, or rewind the
songs, if I choose it.

17

I also have to study all types of music and have a great selection.

I should know the sounds and melodies of music in all sections.

Start by practicing your skills with your family and friends.

Playing bad music at a party can cause it to end.

When booking an event, always know the occasion.
Playing slow music at a kids' party might not fit the equation.

Study these rules, practice, and your career will go far.

Then you can dj like a rock star!

360 Waves

I learned how to do something that every boy craves.

My father taught me how to get 360 waves.

Waves are patterns in your hair that look like water flowing. They get deeper as long as your hair keeps growing.

Before you can get waves, you must cut your hair low.

You must be patient because the results can be slow.

To start the process, there are some things you will need.

A wave brush, shampoo, and conditioner will help you succeed.

You will need hair grease or pomade to give you a look that will thrill.

The final tool is a du rag to help your hair to stay still.

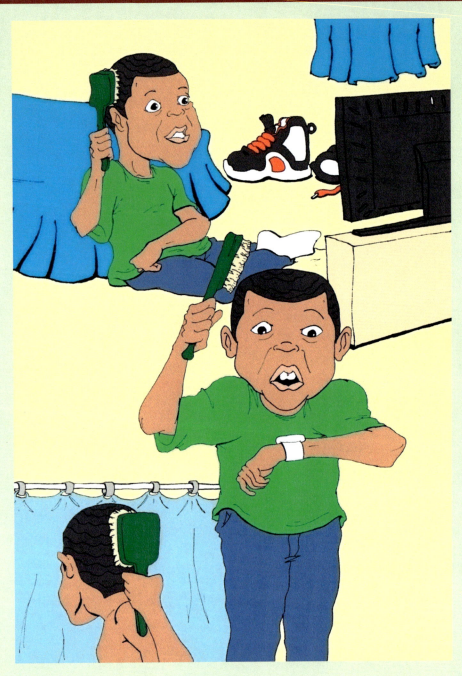

Now that you have everything, you are halfway there.
A towel with hot water on your head will help soften your hair.

Take a small amount of grease and spread it evenly over your head.
If the grease is too heavy, you can use conditioner instead.

You must be willing to brush your hair in a pattern for hours.
Brush if you are watching TV or in the shower.

Brush your hair down in front, behind, and on each side.
This is an important rule that you must abide.

Pay special attention to each individual section.
This will make the waves flow in the 360 degree direction.

You have 360 waves that look like water, where you can go swimming.
With waves like these you'll always feel like you're winning

Bullies are very small, and I'm not talking about size.

They are missing a few things that can't be seen with our eyes.

Bullies try to target people who they think are weak.

They may tease them or push them around, so to speak.

Bullies are sometimes the smart and popular kids.

They try hard to make sure that you have no one to play with.

The truth is that they are jealous of something that you have.

So they pick on you in order to make people laugh.

29

The kids who are picked on may be the ones who are different or

alone. They sometimes are afraid to come outside.

They just want to stay home.

Bullies feel stronger by making others feel small. They are actually

the weakest ones after all.

If you are a witness to bullying, stand up for the bullied person.

Being different makes you special, not a target for hurting.

If you are afraid to step in, tell an adult you trust.

Maybe with a parent or teacher these issues can be discussed.

People are friends with bullies just so that they can fit in.

Those who stand up to bullies are the ones that will really win.

We should practice treating everyone with the utmost respect.

Then this problem with bullying we will finally correct.

Clinton Avenue Crew

Visit www.mcbridestories.com for more titles.

Clinton Avenue Crew

Made in the USA
Middletown, DE
02 July 2022

68282512R00020